# Famous Illustrated
# INDIAN FOLKTALES

**MAPLE KiDS**

**Famous Illustrated**
**INDIAN FOLKTALES**

Published by

MAPLE PRESS PRIVATE LIMITED

Corporate & Editorial Office
A 63, Sector 58, Noida 201 301, U.P., India

phone: +91 120 455 3581, 455 3583
email: info@maplepress.co.in
website: www.maplepress.co.in

Reprinted in 2019

ISBN: 978-93-50336-51-9

Printed at: HT Media Limited, Gr. Noida, India

10 9 8 7 6 5 4 3 2

# Contents

1. Miser Manu ............................................... 4

2. The Cuckoo's Blessings .......................... 11

3. The Day Dreamers ................................... 16

4. The Dutiful Demon ................................. 22

5. The God's Gift ......................................... 28

6. The Horse's Gratitude ........................... 36

7. The Magic of Ninety Nine ..................... 42

8. The Priceless Gem ................................. 47

9. The Saintly Madman .............................. 53

10. The Shadow's Price .............................. 58

11. The Treasure in the Field .................... 63

12. The Unlucky Person ............................. 68

# Miser Manu

Once there lived a merchant named Manu. He was famous in his village for being extremely rich yet being a miser, who did not like to spend anything on anybody, not even on himself!

One afternoon he was coming back from the town after doing his business. On the way he saw a coconut tree full of tender coconuts. As it was a hot day, he felt thirsty. He decided to climb up the coconut tree and get a tender coconut to quench his thirst. He thought, "if he asked anyone to climb up the tree and get a tender coconut, it would cost him money. Instead, if he climbed up himself, he could get the coconut for free". He started climbing the tall tree. By the time he reached its canopy, he was exhausted. When he took a deep breath and looked down, the height from the ground blinded him. He started trembling when he realized that he had climbed so high up in the tree.

The next thought that came to Manu was how to get down to the ground. Forgetting that he had climbed up only to get tender coconuts, he started climbing down. All through, fear gripped him that he may fall down even with one slip. He prayed to God, "Oh God, please help me get to the ground soon and without any mishap."

As he slid down some length, he once again prayed, "God, if you will be by my side as I go down, I'll feed one thousand *brahmins*. This is my vow." Then he realized that he had safely come down half the length of the coconut tree trunk. At this point his miserliness took charge and changing his mind he said to God, "Great God! You've helped me, I know. Till I get to the ground, please be with me. I'll feed at least five hundred *brahmins*."

Then Manu came down further and he changed his vow to feed a "hundred *brahmins*." Again it changed to feeding "ten *brahmins*." When he reached the ground, he settled to "feeding one *brahmin*." He then felt greatly relieved and started for his home.

All the way, he kept thinking, "Hmm, now that I've taken a vow to feed one *brahmin* how much do I need to spend? If I feed a *brahmin* who eats very little I can save my money."

On reaching his village, Manu started looking for a person who ate very little and found a *brahmin* named Thanu. Thanu had heard about Manu's miserliness. So, he was surprised when he was called by Manu for lunch the next day. Thanu, being clever and intelligent, thought, "Hmm, Manu is a miser. If he's calling me for lunch, then I must use this opportunity to get the maximum out of him."

Next morning, Manu left for the town on an urgent business, leaving instructions to his wife to feed Thanu. When Thanu saw Manu leave, he went to his house and said to his wife, "I have just come to enquire if you need any help for preparing the lunch." Manu's wife politely denied any help, but said, "Sir, I'm pleased to have you as our guest. I'd like to know if I need to follow any instructions from you."

Thanu said, "Nothing; just that you must have enough dishes, including a

couple of sweets. I'll go to the temple, do my worship and will come back here in the afternoon."

Thanu left for the temple, and came back by the noon. Manu's wife laid dawn the food on a new silver plate. Thanu looked at the food and said, "Very good! You've prepared the food I like most. But, what about the two gold coins that you need to gift me after I have my food?" Manu's wife was taken aback at this sudden demand. She had not been told about the gift by Manu. Yet she felt that since it was a part of the "*brahmin* feeding ritual", she had to abide by it.

Thanu ate the food offered to him till his stomach was full. Then, whatever food remained he took it all in a bundle and left the place, blessing Manu's wife. As he walked back home, he thought, "Now that I've taken two gold coins from Manu's wife, I'm sure he'll be angry with me. He may even come to take them back. I need to plan accordingly." Thus, on reaching home, he told his wife what she had to do if Manu came to his house, and went in to have a sound sleep.

When Manu returned to his home, his wife told him that Thanu had taken two gold coins as gift. Manu got furious on hearing this and headed straight to Thanu's place.

As planned, Thanu's wife came out of her house and started wailing loudly on seeing Manu.

She cried, "Oh, you cruel person! See what you've done to my husband. He's dying. You've poisoned him. He complained of chest pain after he returned from your place. If anything happens to him, I'll take you to the police and you'll be hanged." Hearing her words, Manu started trembling. He told Thanu's wife, "Why don't you call a doctor now?" Thanu's wife said, "Doctor! Where do I have the money to call a doctor?"

Fearing of the police action and the punishment he may get, Manu said, "Don't worry. Send your son to my place. I'll give him five gold coins. Take your husband to a doctor and get him cured. Please don't go to the police."

Manu felt that by giving so much money, he could save himself from the police at least, even if Thanu died. He took Thanu's son home and handed over five gold coins to him. As the boy ran back to his home, Manu once again prayed to God, "Oh God! Please save me from the gallows. Help Thanu get well. I'll feed one thousand and one *brahmins*."

# The Cuckoo's Blessings

Long ago, in the kingdom of Dharampur, there lived a cuckoo bird called Koyal. She had made her nest on a branch of a banyan tree in the forest adjoining the kingdom. Sitting in her nest, she enchanted the entire kingdom with her melodious voice and sang the whole day. King Dharamvir and his people considered her presence good for the kingdom. This was because, only after she had come to their kingdom that it had prospered, the treasury was always full, there were monsoon rains and greenery abounded everywhere. The king was also a kind and generous ruler.

The forest separated the kingdom of Dharampur from the kingdom of Brahmpur that lay on the opposite side of the forest. It was ruled by King Brahmbhat. Unlike Dharampur, Brahmpur had constant rebellions and outrages by its people. Everyone showed hate, jealousy and suspicion towards each other and indeed the king himself was cruel.

One day, as Brahmbhat went to hunt in the forest, he heard Koyal's voice. He was so mesmerized by it that he decided to have her in his kingdom. He looked around but soon realized that the bird was gone and only her voice was echoing around the trees.

Brahmbhat returned to his palace and called his chief minister. He said, "Today I heard the most enchanting voice of a bird as I went hunting into the forest. The voice was so magical that it still echoes within me. I would like to have that bird in my palace. Find out its whereabouts."

The minister summoned some soldiers and sent them to Dharampur to find out more about Koyal. When the soldiers returned, the minister went to the king and said, "O Majesty, I have come to know that the bird is the lucky charm of the kingdom of Dharampur. It has brought peace, prosperity and happiness to the kingdom."

Brahmbhat grew jealous of Dharampur. He started planning and plotting ways to bring the bird to his palace and make his kingdom prosper. Thus he summoned his minister again and said, "I want the bird immediately. Do something and get the bird from the kingdom. But do it secretly so no one knows of our plan." The minister sent his soldiers to Dharampur again with clear instructions to get Koyal. After a day, the soldiers came back triumphant, bringing along with them the bird that king Brahmbhat desired. As soon as Brahmbhat got Koyal, he put her in a cage made of gold. However, Koyal did not like it, refused to sing or eat, and looked sad.

In Dharampur, the news about Koyal's sudden disappearance spread like wildfire. King Dharamvir sent his men everywhere to search for Koyal. He soon got the news that Koyal had been taken away by Brahmbhat, who was a very cruel, rude and stubborn person. So he called his trusted minister and asked, "Tell me how to bring back Koyal. King Brahmbhat will never consent to give us back our bird. He's very stubborn and I don't want to wage a war with him."

The minister thought for a while and told the king, "O Majesty, near the foot of the hills adjoining the forest, lives an old sage. Brahmbhat goes to the sage to seek his blessings. Let us go to this old wise man and get his advice."

Dharamvir, accompanied by the minister, went to the old sage's hutment. The sage looked at him with surprise and asked, "Mighty king, all my blessings to you. What made you come to me? You've everything in your kingdom. Your people are very happy and satisfied with you. Then why do you need my counsel?"

Dharamvir told the sage, "O revered sire, I'm here to seek your counsel on how to bring back Koyal, my bird. She's like a citizen of my kingdom and her presence enchants us all. Brahmbhat has forcibly taken her to his kingdom." The old sage thought for a while, and said, "Do not worry king Dharamvir, I will get you your Koyal."

In the meanwhile, Brahmbhat was getting disappointed with Koyal. He was puzzled about her quietness. He thought of taking the blessing of the old sage to make Koyal sing. So he went to the sage and told him the entire story.

The Sage thought for a while and asked Brahmbhat, "O king, why did you indeed bring the bird to your kingdom?" The king said, "Sire, I wanted my kingdom to prosper and my people to be happy. Koyal is a lucky charm which has made Dharampur prosperous. May be, by keeping her in Brahmpur, we too shall prosper!"

The old sage snapped, "O you fool! Who told you that the bird is a lucky charm? Now that you have brought the bird, do you think Dhrampur has gone to ruins? It is not in the bird's song but in the king's ability that a country's prosperity depends. It is the goodwill, love and benevolence of a king that makes a country prosper. Go back and hand over Koyal to Dharmpur. She is just a bird who shares the happiness of the people and the king. If you keep her in a cage, she will become dumb. She wants freedom, from you, as well as your corrupt kingdom."

These words of the sage pricked King Brahmbhat and he realized his mistake. He at once ordered his men to take Koyal back to her own natural environment and to be set free in the forest adjoining Dharampur.

# The Day Dreamers

Chandrakant, a farmer, and his wife Supriya were a hard working couple. They tilled the land, sowed the seeds, harvested the crop, and also did some odd jobs to sustain themselves. Their only drawback was that they were both daydreamers. They sometimes even missed on work opportunities due to this habit of theirs.

Once, after finishing a cycle of sowing and harvesting, they both sat for five days chatting and making big plans. Their talk revolved around unreal things or exaggerated fantasies! Once as they sat down to talk, Chandrakant brought up the topic of wanting to become rich through the milk business. He said he wanted to buy a cow. He told Supriya, "If we plan properly and save money from our daily wages, we will be able to buy a cow."

Supriya said, "If I spend only eight rupees a day instead of the present ten, we will save two rupees daily. By the end of the month it will be sixty rupees and at the end of the year we will have seven hundred and twenty rupees with us."

Chandrakant continued, "That means in ten year's time, we can buy a cow." His wife got excited and added, "The price of milk would have also soared by that time. Our 'Lakshmi' will be our lucky charm." Chandrakant asked, "Lakshmi! Who is that?"

Supriya said, "That is the name of our cow. I will take very good care of her, give her the best of cattle feed and keep her healthy always. Then she will reward us with several litres of milk." Chandrakant interfered, "Then that also means, she would need a good living place. I will build her a big shed where she can have enough air and light." Supriya added, "If the shelter is big enough we can milk Lakshmi and arrange to keep the milk in the shed itself before we take it to sell in the market."

Chandrakant was thoughtful for a few moments and then said, "That means we need enough milk pots too. That is also very important, isn't it?" Supriya said, "Ah, yes I forgot this point! We must get good pots as early as possible." The very next day Supriya went and searched the market for pots. She came across good but expensive pots, and brought home six of them. In the evening she showed them all to Chandrakant with pride in her eyes.

Chandrakant asked, "Why have you got six pots?" Supriya explained, "Don't you know how much milk we get from just one cow. We will need one big pot for milk, one pot for curd, one for butter, one for ghee, and one for buttermilk!" Chandrakant was excited about the prospect of becoming rich with just one cow. He appreciated his wife and asked, "I do agree we need five pots for milk and other milk products. What about the sixth my dear? What is that for?"

Supriya innocently said, "Oh dear! What if we get excess milk or any of these products? I will carry anything extra and give it to my brother in the next lane." Chandrakant, on hearing this flared up, "What? You will give it to your brother? With whose permission will you do that?"

Supriya calmly said, "Whose permission do I need to give that extra pot with milk or curd to my brother?" Chandrakant retorted, "Have you gone mad? I work hard and save the money, buy the cow, build her the shed, give her good feed, make her healthy and milk her. Why should you then give that excess to your brother who does not give us anything?"

This argument went on for over an hour with heated exchange of words. Finally, Chandrakant lost his temper and smashed all the pots by hurling them down. He then asked Supriya, "Now that I have broken them all, how will you take the excess milk or curd to you brother?" Supriya started wailing at the top of her voice at this. All this time, their neighbour Makarand was listening to their conversation. He was wise and good at reasoning and logic. He waited quietly, but when he heard Supriya crying, he thought it was time for him to interfere. He came to Chandrakant's home and asked him what the argument was about.

Chandrakant, still in the day dreaming state, said, "See, my wife wants to give away the excess milk and curd to her brother!" Makarand was confused and asked, "Milk? Which milk?" Chandrakant continued, "The milk from our cow Lakshmi."

Makarand rolled his eyes here and there, looking for the cow. He then asked Chandrakant, "But where is the cow?" Still unable to connect with reality, Chandrakant said "I meant the cow we will buy in ten years time."

That was the height of stupidity, and Makarand lost his patience. He immediately thought of an idea to bring Chandrakant and his wife to their senses quickly. He said, "Ah, I see! I had been wondering all these days about who damages my vegetable farm.

It must be your cow Lakshmi. She sneaks into the garden at night and plunders it. As the owner of the cow, you deserve punishment for that."

So saying, Makarand picked up a thick stick kept in the corner of Chandrakant's house and started beating Chandrakant black and blue. As it started to pain him, Chandrakant came back to reality and asked Makarand, "Why are you beating me? You have no vegetable farm." Makarand replied, "Why did you break the pots? You have no cow either."

Supriya, hearing this conversation, started laughing with embarrassment. She realized her's as well as her husband's stupidity. Chandrakant too felt ashamed of his act and Makarand now asked Chandrakant to forgive him for taking such a drastic step!

The couple stopped daydreaming from that day onwards.

# The Dutiful Demon

In a remote village of the Baharaich district, lived a rich farmer named Manoharbhan. He possessed a huge cattle farm, a palatial house with a big garden, besides several acres of farmland. To look after these he had appointed many servants. He paid his servants a meagre salary and did not treat them will. His wife and children disliked this, but did not have the courage to say so.

One day, Manoharbhan was sitting watching his servants' work, when suddenly he had an idea. He wanted to save as much money as possible and the best way for this would be to dismiss all the servants and appoint just one able person who could look after everything.

He called his wife and discussed this idea with her. She told him, "Dear, now that is not fair! Already those servants are under paid. They are working for us out of compulsion. They have their families with them and so cannot go far away to earn their living. If you remove them from work, they will live in poverty." She pleaded with him to not dismiss them from work. But Manoharbhan ignored her plea saying, "If I give them work and keep paying them, I will myself become a pauper one day. All my money is wasted on these servants. I need just one person who can do all the work."

Having decided thus, Manoharbhan pondered on how to look for a person who can do all his jobs. Where would he find such a person? If only he had the Aladdin's lamp, he could rub it and summon a genie whom he could have as his servant. Then he thought, "Why not go to the old sage at the mountain foothills? Perhaps he can give me a genie by his meditative powers. Then I can have the genie as my servant, free of cost!"

This idea suited him well and he headed to the foothills of the mountains. There he found the old sage. After paying his respects, he put forward his desire to the sage. The old sage could read his mind. He understood that Manoharbhan was a miser and that he underpaid his servants. He wanted to teach him a lesson. So he told Manobharhan, "My son, I can understand your idea. I can provide you a servant who is very dutiful. He can do as many tasks as you give him, free of cost. Only that, you need to keep giving him work. Otherwise he will get bored and eat you." Manoharbhan agreed to this readily as he had plenty of work at his farms and at his home. Then the old sage meditated and uttered some words, and with a thundering sound, appeared a bald headed strong man with a big moustache. He paid his respects to the sage and his new master Manoharbhan. Pleased at this new prospect, Manoharbhan took his demon servant home. He summoned all his other servants and declared, "Look here, all of you. Whatever you people have been doing for me, will now be done by this one person, that too without any payment. I do not require any of your services hereafter." The servants, feeling sad and cheated, left Manoharbhan.

Soon, the demon took over the entire charge. Manoharbhan gave him general instructions to look after his fields, his farms, his gardens as well as all his household work. To start with, Manoharbhan told the demon, "Go and clean the garden that is full of dry leaves. Then prune the plants and shrubs, and water them too." Manoharbhan thought that he had given enough work to the demon for the day. He expected these tasks to tire the demon soon. So, with these thoughts, Manoharbhan went off to sleep.

Just ten minutes later the demon came and

woke him up saying, "Master! Master! Get up."
Manoharbhan got up and asked the demon, "Why
have you woken me up?" The demon replied,
"Master, I have done all the tasks you gave me for
the garden. Tell me what else I should do?"

Surprised at his speed, Manoharban went to
the garden to see for himself. The demon had
made it very beautiful in that short span of time!
Unbelievable as it was, Manoharbhan now told
him, "Go and plough the fields, remove the weeds
and sow new seeds in the vacant plots of land."
The demon went away to do these tasks, while
his master again lay down to rest. Manoharbhan
would not have slept for even ten minutes when
the demon again woke him up. The demon said,
"Master! I've done all the work in the fields.
What next?"

Amazed, Manoharbhan now told the demon to
clean the house. The demon did this too in a short
span of time. Absolutely confused, and frightened,
Manoharbhan felt it necessary to think of some new
task for the demon, otherwise he would be eaten up
by him as advised by the sage. He thought, "I should
outsmart this demon. Let me find a solution to my
problem." Manoharbhan finally got an idea. He
pointed to his pet dog and said, "Go and straighten
the tail of that dog."

The demon went to the dog and got into the

impossible task of straightening its tail. Every time he straightened it, it got curled again. In the meantime, the dog got provoked and started barking loudly at the demon. The demon got startled and terrified by this reaction of the dog, took to his heels and ran away to the distant forest; never to return.

Manoharbhan took a sigh of relief and thanked the Almighty for saving him from the "dutiful demon."

# The God's Gift

In a village in Madhya Pradesh lived a poor *brahmin* named Vibhoothi. He earned his living by performing yagnas and *poojas* at the homes of his patrons. His profession fetched him very little money. He found it difficult to raise four children with the money he earned and wished to find some way to increase his income. He thought for many years but did not come upon any idea.

Frustrated by his poverty, Vibhoothi decided to meditate upon Lord Shiva as a last resort. He sincerely believed that his devoutness will definitely fetch him a reward from the Great Lord. He went to the forest and found a secluded spot. There he sat down and started his mediation. After several days, Lord Shiva appeared before Vibhoothi, pleased by his devotion. Vibhoothi bowed to Lord Shiva, who asked him, "Son, What shall I do for you?"

Vibhoothi replied, "O great God, please give me a magical pot as a gift. The pot should be always full of grains. It should get replenished and should never become empty. That way I will at least be assured of regular meals for my family."

Lord Shiva smiled and said, "I praise your smartness and devotion to your family. You did not ask for gold, silver or wealth. You've just asked for a pot of grains. Here it is. Keep it safely and get benefitted by it."

So saying, Lord Shiva disappeared. Vibhoothi was very pleased that his wish had finally been granted. He started on his way back home with the pot. He had barely travelled half the way when the sun went down and it was dark all around. Vibhoothi thought it would be safer to travel during the day, when he will not lose the path nor get robbed by the bandits. He saw a light in some distance, and nearing it found that it came from a house. The house belonged to a merchant, and Vibhoothi decided to take shelter at his place.

Vibhoothi stayed there overnight, clinging to his pot tightly. The merchant observed this and asked him, "Sir, it seems there is something special about this pot. Why are you keeping it close to your body at all times? Why don't you keep it in a corner and take it with you in the morning when you leave?"

Vibhoothi said, "Sir, you don't know the value of this pot. It possesses magical powers to replenish the grain in it every time the grains are emptied. This is a gift to me from Lord Shiva to save me from my abject poverty. I will use some grains to feed my family. The rest I will sell in the market and earn some money!"

As the merchant listened to Vibhoothi, he wanted to steal the pot from him so he could do business with the grains and reap benefit from it. When Vibhoothi slept, he quietly replaced it with another pot of his own that was similar in appearance. The next morning Vibhoothi took this new pot with him and returned to his home.

His wife and children were very happy to see him back. Vibhoothi related his extraordinary experience to them and gave the pot to his wife. She was very eager to see its magic. She upturned it to see if it provided the grains and also got filled with new grains. But alas! She was shocked to find that no magic happened and concluded that it was an ordinary pot.

Disappointed, Vibhoothi pondered for a week why the pot did not yield the grains since it was given by Lord Shiva himself. Yet he needed the solution to his problem somehow, and decided to go back to the forest and start his penance again. This time too, Lord Shiva appeared before him. On seeing him, Vibhoothi asked with dejection in his tone, "What wrong have I done for you to not grant me my wish Lord? If you did not want me to get rid of my poverty, you could have just told me so and I would have accepted it as your command. I have no use for the pot you gave me since it gives me no grains. It is just an ordinary pot."

Lord Shiva calmed him down and said, "Son, what I gave you was a magical pot indeed. It was replaced by the merchant who hosted you, with a similar looking pot. He cheated on you. I am giving you another pot now. Take this to the merchant and tell him that it is magical. Then see what happens."

Vibhoothi did as Lord Shiva advised him. He told the merchant, "Sir, the pot I got last time turned out to be an ordinary one. So God has blessed me with a new pot. This is more precious than the previous one and has better magical powers." Saying this, Vibhoothi went off to sleep. The merchant again secretly took the pot. He became so eager and restless to test its magic that he opened it immediately. Out jumped several scorpions, and started stinging the merchant. Hearing the merchant yell, Vibhoothi got up and looked at him. He understood the situation. The merchant asked for Vibhoothi's forgiveness and to pardon him for stealing his magical pot.

Vibhoothi took his original magic pot from the merchant and returned home with both the magical pots, the one with the grains and the one with the scorpions. His wife and children were very happy to see him with the magic pots. From that day, they used the grains' pot to eat well and to sell the excess grains in the market. The family became well to do and lived a happy life. The pot with the scorpions' was kept covered, high on a shelf where only Vibhoothi could reach with his height.

But this happiness came to an end when, one day while playing, Vibhoothi's children knocked the grains' pot off its shelf and broke it into pieces. Vibhoothi was shattered and spent a sleepless night. His wife urged him to go and pray to Lord Shiva again. Heeding her advice, Vibhoothi went to the forest to mediate once more.

After some days, the God appeared before him. Vibhoothi kneeled before him and said, "Dear God, I ask once again for your help. The magic pot you gave me is now broken. I have no other means to drive away my poverty." Lord Shiva took pity on him and gave him yet another pot and said, "This is the last time you will get a pot. Keep it safe and it will help you lead a life without poverty."

Vibhoothi thanked the Lord and went back to his house. He and his wife opened the pot and found mouth watering sweets inside. Vibhoothi's wife suggested to him, "Why not open a sweet shop in our village? We will be able to make a good profit from that." The sweets that came out from the pot were so delicious that the entire village came to Vibhoothi's shop to buy them. Soon, the family became rich!

The head of the village came to know about Vibhoothi's magic pot and thought of wielding his power to possess it. Then he decided against it and instead hatched another ploy. He called Vibhoothi and said, "Brother, I would like to borrow your pot for a day. I came to know about the sweets that come out of it. I have got some special guests coming tomorrow, and would like to offer these magical sweets to them. Can you lend me the pot for a day?"

Since he was the village head, Vibhoothi could not deny him his request. So he brought the pot and gave it to him. After a day or two, when the village head had not returned the pot, Vibhoothi went to get it back himself. The village head looked blankly at him and said, "Pot! Magical pot? When did you give it to me? Are you in your right mind?"

Stunned, Vibhoothi caught onto his trick, and quietly walked back home. He thought for a while and prayed to the God for a solution. Just then he remembered the other pot gifted to him by Lord Shiva. He took that pot straight to the village head and opened its lid. Out came thousands of scorpions which sprawled across the village head's house, chasing him. The village head ran straight up to Vibhoothi, asked him for forgiveness, and handed him over his original magic pot.

Thereafter, Vibhoothi and his family lived a happy and prosperous life using the power of the magic pot.

# The Horse's Gratitude

Hargobind was a poor farmer. He lived in a village near Jalandhar in Punjab with his wife. They had no children. He worked for the village's richest landlord and earned a small income. With meagre earnings, it was difficult for him to make both ends meet. To supplement the income, his wife too made her contribution of work to run the family by stitching clothes for village children.

One day, Hargobind received a message from his aunt, his late father's sister and the only surviving relative of that generation. She lived alone in another village about hundred miles away. She was very old and very rich. However, she was also a miser and never bothered to entertain any relatives or well-wishers in her house. With her advancing years, she was becoming weak and unable to take care of herself. As days went by, she had felt it necessary to have someone take care of her, since she felt she was approaching her death fast. She remembered Hargobind as a kind and caring person, and thus sent word to him to come and meet her.

Hargobind realized that his aunt must be terribly ill, which must have made her send for him. In all the previous years, he had not heard from her even once. He left his home and walked to reach his aunt's village. On the way he wondered what she would say when they met! As he neared his aunt's village, he met a washer-man, and asked the directions to his aunt's house. The washer-man looked surprisingly at him and said, "Do you really want to go to that old woman? What is wrong with you?" Hargobind said, "She is my aunt and has herself sent a word for me to meet her."

The washer-man said, "Really! It is nice of you to come. Nobody else would do this for a person like her. She never entertains anyone in her home and is a terrible miser. No one dares to pass by her house or pet her horse, for fear of being shooed away."

Hargobind smiled at him and made his way towards his aunt's house. After some search, he located it at the end of a secluded lane. The house was in a very run down

condition with rubbish strewn around, uncut grass in the lawn, and the walls wearing a dirty look.

Hargobind wondered how anyone could live in such a house. As he was thinking this, his eyes fell upon a horse tied to a pole near the gate. The horse was lean and weak, as if he had not eaten for many days. The pathetic condition of the horse moved Hargobind. He felt sorry for the animal, and went to the nearest hay seller to bring the horse a bundle of hay. As he fed the horse, it hurried up to eat the hay and Hargobind felt there was a reflection of thankfulness in it's eyes. Then it began to neigh.

Just at that moment, hearing the neighing sound, Hargobind's aunt came out. She could not recognize him, and started scolding him, "Hey, you! Why have you come here? I've nothing to give you." Hargobind hurriedly said, "No, no, aunt, it's me, Hargobind."

Still, the old lady did not seem to be happy to see her visitor. She said, "Oh! Yes, Hargobind, it's nice that you've come before my death. I have called you for an important work. See, here's my horse which is costing me too much. I cannot feed it anymore. Take it with you and consider it as property inherited from me. He may be of some use to you."

Hargobind took a deep breath at the appalling attitude of his aunt. But, since he had already developed a soft corner for the horse, he readily agreed and took it back to his village. When

Hargobind narrated everything to his wife, she too took pity on the horse and said, "Let us take care of him like our own child." And so in a few days, with enough love and care, the horse put on weight and started looking healthy.

After a few weeks, the news of his aunt's death reached Hargobind. Hargobind rode on his horse, who was now completely strong and agile, and reached her place. After the last rites of his aunt, Hargobind decided to leave the place. As he rode a few steps, his horse stopped suddenly at one place. All efforts of Hargobind to make the animal move seemed futile. Patting him gently, Hargobind asked "My dear, what is wrong with you? Why don't you want to come with me?"

So saying, he even tried to kick the horse to make it move. Instead, the horse started going round and round at that particular spot and kept circling it. Then, bending it's neck, it touched the ground with its nose, it began to neigh.

Suddenly it occurred to Hargobind that the horse might be conveying a message to him. He brought a spade from inside the house and started digging the ground. Soon, his spade hit on some metal. When Hargobind cleared the mud off the place, he found a big trunk. He opened it, and to his surprise, he found diamonds, gold coins and silver wares in the trunk. Right in front of his eyes was everything that could make him and his successive generations lead a rich and prosperous life.

When Hargobind brought the trunk home, his wife too could not believe her eyes at first. They both thanked the horse and the almighty for this fortune. Thereafter, they lived a happy and prosperous life for many years to come, in which time they had two beautiful children. Yet they looked after the horse with the same love and care as they had given him before, and also gave charity to the poor and the needy from their riches.

# The Magic of Ninety Nine

In a village lived two men, Samu and Somu. They were neighbours, with their houses separated by just a barbed fence. Samu was rich and economically much better off than Somu. Yet he spent very little, even on his family's needs, and never entertained any guests. On the other hand, Somu worked hard day and night; earning just enough to make both ends meet. Inspite of his poor status, he led a happy, contented life. He was always visited by friends and well-wishers, which kept a festive spirit alive in his house.

Samu's wife always wondered how Somu's family could be happy despite a small income. She was always surprised to see lots of people around Somu's family, enjoining and celebrating with them. One day, she decided to find out the secret of this happiness. She visited Somu's house and asked his wife, "Dear friend, can I ask you about a secret?" Somu's wife was surprised and said, "Secret? We do not have any secret, but please ask what you want to know." Samu's wife continued, "I find you people always happy and contented. How is it possible for you to be this way, even though you need to work hard to earn money?" Somu's wife simply replied with a smile, "Friend, I really don't know the reason why."

This did not satisfy Samu's wife's curiosity. She came back to her house and started thinking about this. When Samu came back home in the evening, he saw a thoughtful frown on his wife's forehead and asked, "Dear, what is wrong with you? Is something worrying you?" His wife said, "Dear, I'm not worried. I'm just trying to find out a secret. I am trying to determine the secret of the happiness of our neighbour!"

Samu paused for a while and then said, "Dear, you know, it's just that they have not been affected by the magic of ninety-nine!" His wife asked, "Magic of ninety-nine? What is that?" Samu said, "Dear, just give me some time. I'll show you how the magic of ninety nine affects Somu's family."

Saying this, Samu went to take bath before the dinner, leaving his wife wondering about his words. Days went by and slowly Samu's wife observed a change in Somu's family. She could hardly see Somu and his wife come out to sit and chat happily. Also, the visitors to their place had reduced considerably. There seemed to be no happiness on Somu or his wife's faces. The festive spirit of their house was also gone.

When she could no longer contain herself, Samu's wife went to Somu's place to find out the reason for this sudden change. After some hesitation, Somu's wife shared the cause of her worry with Samu's wife. She said, "Friend, you know how happy and contended we were. Now the "magic of ninety-nine" is ruining our lives."

Samu's wife asked, "Magic of ninety-nine? Tell me more about it."

Somu's wife continued, "A month ago, when my husband was returning home, he found a bag full of silver coins near our gate. He brought it home and enquired about it to me. When I said I didn't know anything about it, he opened it and counted the coins. There were ninety-nine coins in that bag. We thought that if we added one more coin, the total coins will be rounded off to a hundred, and would become a good saving for our future. From the very next day, we started cutting down our expenses, stopped entertaining guests and somehow managed to earn one silver coin. We added it to the ninety-nine coins and were relieved."

At this Samu's wife interjected, "Now that you have saved hundred coins why do you still seem worried?" Somu's wife said heaving, "Again the magic of ninety-nine!"

Puzzled, Samu's wife looked at Somu's wife who continued, "The very next day my husband come back from work and said that since we have a hundred coins now, it would be nice if we saved another hundred and make it two hundred. From that day onwards, our worries have started again."

Somu's wife finished her story and Samu's wife left the place quietly. Samu who had been listening to them from behind the door smiled and thought to himself, "That's the magic of the ninety nine coins I left at their door!"

# The Priceless Gem

Shyamlal, a poor land tiller, worked for the village head. He was honest and hard working, and was content with whatever little money he got in return for his labour. In fact, while other workers got their wages in cash, he got things like grains or pulses as his wage. These he would then barter in the market for the things he wanted for his family, so he never knew the value of money. As for taking a day off from his work, he never yearned for it.

One day, his employer, the rich village head called him and said, "Shyamlal, you are very different from others, honest and simple. This way you will never became rich or satisfy your family's needs. Now, there is a fair put up in the neighbouring village. I'll give you a hundred rupees this time for wage. Go to the fair and get whatever your wife and son ask from you. Make them happy. Today will be an off day for you from work."

Shyamlal was pleasantly surprised at this. He went to his wife and told her about it. She said, "Very well, get me something

that will beautify me." Then Shyamlal went to his son and asked what he wanted. His son said, "Father, get me something to play with."

Shyamlal reached the fair and looked around. He saw shops selling bags, slippers, cosmetics and sarees. He decided to get a saree for his wife. He went to the shop and asked the shopkeeper to show him the best of the sarees. The shopkeeper displayed the best sarees in his shop for Shyamlal to choose from.

Shyamlal decided on one saree and asked the shopkeeper for its price. The shopkeeper asked him to pay five hundred rupees. Shyamlal showed him the hundred rupee note and asked, "Sir, is this enough?" Annoyed at this, the shopkeeper shouted at him, "Hey, are you joking? I want five notes of this kind." Shyamlal did not understand the shopkeeper and replied, "I've only one of this kind of notes. Can't you adjust with just one?" Irritated, the shopkeeper drove him out of the shop.

Shyamlal then went to a toy shop and looked for a wooden horse for his son. He found one and asked the shopkeeper for its price. The shopkeeper said, "Sir, it is two hundred rupees." Shyamlal gave him the hundred rupee note he had and said, "I've only one of this kind of notes. Can you give me the toy, taking this note?" The shopkeeper was very upset at this, and pushed Shyamlal out of the shop, saying,

"Do not ever think of coming back here!"

Dejected, Shyamlal went back with the money and reached home. This wife and son were excited on his return, and asked him, "What have you bought for us?" Shyamlal hung his head and said, "The shopkeepers did not take my money in return for their things." Shyamlal's wife asked, "How can they reject your money?" Shyamlal explained, "They said, they need some more money for the silk saree and the wooden horse."

Beating her forehead, Shyamlal's wife said, "How senseless you are to demand a silk saree and a wooden horse for just hundred rupees! Please don't show your face to me. Go away." While Shyamlal left his house and went to the river bank to take some rest, his wife went straight to his employer and related the entire incident. She requested him to make her husband sensible.

The next morning when Shyamlal went to his work, his employer told him, "Go and dig a well in our field. This work you should do entirely on your own. Then only you'll come to your senses."

As Shyamlal started digging a well, he hit his spade on a brass pot. He took it out and found some shining pieces, which he thought were stones. He took the brass pot to his master and asked "Master, I found this pot of stones in your field while digging the well. What shall I do with it?"

In anger, the employer snapped at him, "Go and eat the stones Shyamlal!" Shyamlal tried biting into one stone, but it was too hard to be bitten into. Not knowing what to do next, Shyamlal decided to take the pot to the market. There he went to a person who sold diamonds. He asked the shopkeeper, "Sir, would you like to have some shining stones?" Surprised, the shopkeeper asked him to show the stones. After seeing them, he called up his assistant and secretly sent him out on some pretext.

The shopkeeper then kept Shyamlal busy in some conversation, and in the meanwhile, his assistant arrived with the king's men. They arrested Shyamlal on seeing him in possession of the brass pot with diamonds in it!

On being produced in front of the king, Shyamlal trembled and said, "Your Majesty, I did not do anything wrong but your men think I'm a robber. Please do justice." The king called his minister and whispered to him, "This is the same man I saw in my dream. God has ordered me to help him." Then to Shyamlal the king said with a smile, "Don't' be afraid of me, Shyamlal. I came to know that you wanted to get a silk saree for your wife and a wooden horse for your son. They are now ready. You may take them with you as my gift. It is God's command I'm following."

Shyamlal asked, "But sir, why did the shopkeeper call for your men on looking at these shining stones I had?" The king said, "Shyamlal, they are not just shining stones. They are diamonds worth several thousand rupees!" Shyamlal innocently told the king, "O Majesty, would you mind exchanging these stones for the gifts you're going to give me?" The king was totally taken aback to see such an honest man. He said, "No Shyamlal, these diamonds are yours for ever, and also these gifts."

Shyamlal folded his hands, bowed to the king and said, "Your Majesty, these diamonds will be worthy for those who know their value. For me, hard work is the most precious gem. I have my hands and feet with which I can work hard. Then what is the need for these diamonds?" Saying this, Shyamlal left the palace with people standing around watching him with amazement and awe.

On hearing about this, Shyamlal's wife cried with joy and pride. When he reached home, she and his son both hugged him and said, "We are really proud of you!"

# The Saintly Madman

Long ago, in a kingdom by the Tapti River in Southern India, there lived a saint. He had many followers, not only in the kingdom where he lived, but also in the neighbouring kingdoms. People believed that he had miraculous powers with which he could heal anyone, and also provide a solution to any problem. He was also respected for his wisdom. The king himself consulted him and took his blessings and opinion before taking any crucial decisions related with the kingdom.

Being a saint, he was invited by many rich men to their dwellings to bless them. He gave discourses to large gatherings, and in essence, he was regarded as being next to God himself, as far as the people's faith in him was concerned. In such a scenario, the saint got less time to devote to meditation or prayers, but started accumulating wealth through his rich followers.

The saint constantly took pilgrimages to holy cities where he was met with and honoured by his devotees. He used to initially walk across forests, up the mountains and through

shallow river beds. This kept him healthy and fresh. But as his popularity spread, his wealthy devotees arranged for a palanquin and some bearers to carry him everywhere. Slowly, though he was cut off from nature, the saint started enjoying the comfort of moving around in the palanquin all the time.

Once, as he was coming back from a neighbouring kingdom, with a procession of devotees in front of his palanquin, the bearers suddenly stopped moving. As the saint looked out, he saw a shabby looking man wearing unclean and torn clothes. He had a long beard with dishevelled hair. On the whole, he looked like a madman. Though the palanquin bearers tried to drive him away, he did not move an inch. The saint opened the curtains of the palanquin to take a closer look at this dishevelled person. He then stopped his bearers and said, "Let me hear what this man has to say. He must be yearning to see me. May be, he needs my blessings."

Then he called the madman near him and asked, "My son, tell me why you stopped my palanquin? What do you want from me?" The madman said, "Dear master, people call me mad. But I don't know why? I came to meet you and get some help."

The saint looked puzzled. He asked the man, "Tell me my son, what I can do for you? Do you want to be cured of your madness, or would you like to become rich?" The madman said, "Nothing of these, O great sire. People tell me that you know where heaven is, where God is. Please tell me where they are and how I can reach there?"

The saint was dumb-founded. He had to give a convincing reply to the madman; else people would not respect him. He closed his eyes, thought for a while and said to the madman, "Go and stand in the centre of where the four roads meet. Close your eyes, raise both your hands, and think about God. Then start praying to him. God himself will come and take you to his heaven." This answer convinced the madman and he gave way to the palanquin bearers to continue their journey. The saint also felt relieved that the madman had left him unhurt. Soon he forgot about this incident.

Some days later, the saint was again called by one of his wealthy disciples in the neighbouring kingdom for a religious ritual. As usual, he rode in his palanquin, with a procession of his followers in the front. The procession reached the same place where he had met the madman some days ago. As the place was on the outskirts of the town, it bore a deserted look. The procession then reached the place where the four roads met and suddenly stopped there.

The saint peeped out to see why the procession had stopped. To his surprise, there stood the madman, his eyes closed, hands raised upwards, as if in deep meditation. The saint now remembered the previous incident with the madman, including the fact that he himself had advised the madman to stand there in that posture so as to go to heaven.

Taken aback, the saint thought, "This man has believed me. He trusts that God will come to take him to the heaven. He must be really mad." As the saint was mulling this idea, there was a sudden flash of light from above, and a glowing figure descended towards the earth from the sky. It held the madman by his raised hands and started lifting him upwards towards the heaven. In a sudden realization, the saint understood the truth of life! He quickly jumped out of his palanquin and caught hold of the madman by his legs. The people standing there were stunned and shouted, "O sire, why are you holding on to him? Leave him!"

The saint replied back, "No, he is a true devotee and God has acknowledged it. That is why God himself has descended specially to take the man to heaven. All along, I had preached on philosophy and spiritualism, but never really practiced any of those. Let me accept my failure. If I don't go with him to heaven today, I will never reach God. His single-minded devotion has taught me the true value of life."

So saying, the saint, holding on to the madman, rose towards the abode of God.

# The Shadow's Price

Bimal Sagar was the head of a remote village in the Satara district of Maharashtra. He was the richest man in his village, with several acres of land, a palatial house and a pig farm. He also proclaimed himself to be the owner of the only peepal tree in the village. He called it his own because it stood next to the wall of his house. People of the village dared not question this premise for fear of his power and an attitude for revenge. He laid dawn rules for the villagers and even took the authority upon himself to punish the 'offenders'.

One day Raju, the village washerman was walking with his donkey back from the river. It was a hot afternoon. He had washed and dried the clothes and was coming back to distribute them to the villagers. He handed over Bimal Sagar's clothes in his house, and as he came out, his eyes caught the shadow of the peepal tree sprawling on the ground. This tempted him to have a short nap in the shadow. He stretched himself on the ground and soon started snoring.

After some time, he heard a man's voice yelling at him, "Hey you! What are you doing here? How dare you use my tree's shadow without my permission?" Raju opened his eyes

and found the owner of the voice to be Bimal Sagar. Shaken by the rough voice, Raju took a pause and then told Bimal Sagar, "Please forgive me lord. It is so hot. I just wanted to sit here for sometime but I don't know how I snoozed off."

Bimal Sagar said, "Just get away from here. This place is mine. I cannot see anyone using my place like this." Raju tried to explain, "But sir, I had been working for you for several years. What harm did I bring by using this shadow?"

This question awakened something in Bimal Sagar. He thought, "Hmm, Raju is right. But if I give him the privilege today, then he may expect it tomorrow, day after, or forever. Then other people also may start using it. No, I should not show this generosity." He then told Raju, "Look, I don't want your explanations. I cannot let other person use any of my things free of cost."

Startled, Raju asked, "Sir, what do you mean? Do you expect me to pay you for using the shadow?" Bimal Sagar firmly said, "Yes, of course." Raju said,

"Ok sir, tell me how much I need to pay?" Bimal Sagar said, "One thousand rupees for a month from today." Raju, on hearing this, started planning about how to teach Bimal Sagar a lesson. Then he told him, "Ok sir, I will get you the money."

Bimal Sagar was pleased as this meant an additional income from a property that was not of his own making. He thought this business would be very good.

Raju went to his house and told his wife, "Dear, please give me your ornaments. I need to pledge them for an urgent business. I will return them to you after a few days." Raju's wife was surprised at this but knowing her husband to be a wise man, she trusted him and gave away her ornaments quietly. Raju took them to the goldsmith for pledging.

He got some money from the goldsmith against the ornaments, and took the money to Bimal Sagar. They both signed a deed of this deal. From then on, Raju made it a routine to use the peepal's shadow as his resting place whenever he wanted. Then one fine day Raju was not to been seen. He was not there even the next day, and the whole of another week.

Bimal Sagar felt elated at his double bonus, getting the money from Raju without his using the shadow. But his happiness was short lived.

One afternoon when Bimal Sagar came back from his business, he saw a big crowd under the peepal tree. Raju was standing in the shadow of the peepal tree with his friends and relatives. Shocked, Bimal Sagar asked him, "Hey you! Why have you brought all these people to my place? I sold the shadow of the Peepal tree just to you. But now you and your family are trying to occupy the land too that is near the tree."

Raju explained calmly, "Master, I do agree that you sold me the tree's shadow. But if you find your land around it is being occupied, better remove your land and keep it elsewhere."

Stunned at this reply, Bimal Sagar said in a confused tone, "Why don't you take away your shadow?" The crowd of people around them laughed at this foolishness and Raju said, "Sure master, then I will have to cut the peepal tree and take it with me."

Bimal Sagar had no words to say any further. He could not allow the peepal tree, which had been there for several years, to be cut. He accepted his mistake to Raju and gave him back his money. Raju returned home and gave back his wife all her ornaments as he had promised her.

# The Treasure in the Field

In a village situated in a remote corner of India, lived a farmer with his four sons. The farmer was very hard working and managed his family well. As he grew old, he felt the need to ensure that his sons followed his ways to become hardworking and responsible too.

Unfortunately, his sons were totally irresponsible. They never showed interest in their father's farmland or farming. They wanted a work which required minimum effort. Slowly, as the old farmer became weak, his farmlands were ignored by his sons. The lands became dry and barren. The farmer, worried at this development, called his friend and discussed the matter with him. The friend gave him a good idea to make his sons take up the farm work.

Accordingly, the old man called his sons the next day and said, "My sons, I am growing old and weak. I no more have the strength to do farming or leave any property for you. But I can tell you one secret with which

you can become rich." The lazy sons took interest in the old man's words and eagerly waited for him to proceed.

The old man continued, "My sons, I recently came to know the secret from my friend whose father was a good friend of my father. He said that some treasure was hidden in our farm but no one knew where in the farm it was buried. I tried my best to search for it, but without success. It is now for you to find the treasure. Also, after my death, all four of you should remain united. Whatever you get from our land, you all should share it equally!"

The four sons were very happy to hear about the treasure and they promised their father that they would share everything equally among themselves.

Some days later the old farmer died. The four sons had already started digging the field, working day and night in search of the treasure. For several days they dug the field and did not leave any corner. Yet they could not find the treasure. They felt disheartened. But due to all their digging efforts the field looked well ploughed. They grudgingly sowed the seeds that were in their house from the last season's harvest. Because of all their digging, the soil had turned fertile, and they had a good crop that harvest season. They reaped so much profit that they decided to celebrate it with a meal for the entire village.

A day was fixed for celebration. They called all their friends, relatives, neighbours and village folk and served them a sumptuous lunch. It was during this time that they met their father's friend too. Though they had stopped looking for it, yet they had not forgotten about the treasure, it was still raging in their mind! They were waiting for an opportunity to share their grief and concern with their father's friend. So when he arrived for the lunch, they took him aside to clarify their doubts.

Their father's friend told them, "Why, you young men! I'm proud to find you all well settled in your work. If only your father had been alive, he would have been happy to find you rich and prosperous."

The eldest of the four brothers said,

"Uncle, we do agree that our father wanted us all to become responsible and rich. But, if we had been able to locate the treasure we would not have to do the hard work on the fields. That would have been much better."

Now came the moment for their father's friend to clarify. He said, "Exactly, my dear sons! Your father indeed wanted you all to take up farming and become responsible. And you have really got your treasure!"

Confused, the second son said, "But, uncle, where is the treasure? We found no pot or chest of gold coins. All our efforts of digging the entire field went in vain."

The father's friend clarified, "That is it son. You dug the entire field in search of a treasure which was never there! If only you were asked to do the work without the lure of the treasure, none of you would have worked to make the land fertile. If you had not made it fertile, you would not have got a good harvest. If there was no harvest, you would not have heaped profits. Has your field not given you this treasure? What else do you want? You must be thankful to your father for making you realize the worth of hard work. This is the treasure that he wanted you to look for."

As he finished this the sons felt guilty for having wanted an easy life and overnight success. They realized they had been given the treasure of goodwill, hardwork and responsibility. They asked their father's friend to forgive them and promised him that they would take good care of their field and remain united always.

Their father smiled from the heaven on hearing this!

# The Unlucky Person

King Samudrasuman ruled the vast kingdom of Patliputra and its adjoining areas. He was righteous and noble, and took good care of his subjects. Everyone respected him and held him high in esteem for his good qualities. The only thing that ailed the king was his superstitious beliefs. Even the courtiers were not spared of its ill effects. There was only one courtier who could tackle the situation whenever the king brought forth a superstitious belief. It was the royal priest assigned for the religious ceremonies.

The most alarming of Samudrasuman's superstitions was the belief that whoever he saw first on waking up daily, that person would be responsible for everything that happened to him that day. The person who brought good luck would be considered auspicious by the king and rewarded. But if on meeting a person, he had a bad day, the person was sure to be punished the very next morning. The punishment ranged with the severity of 'bad luck', from whippings to banishment from the kingdom.

Thus everyone, from the maids to the ministers, thought twice before going in front of the king for any official work in the morning. However when the king himself called his attendants for some work, he

disregarded his own superstition. They also left him alone for his morning walks in the royal gardens, not wanting to be the first ones whom the king saw on any day.

One day, Samudrasuman slept later than usual and got up late the next morning. The royal priest had already arrived at the palace and had gone to the garden to get fresh flowers for the *pooja*. As he was plucking flowers, Samudrasuman arrived there for his morning walk. The priest could not avoid the sight of the king, and went to greet him.

The royal priest was not only wise but also known for his wit and humour. Before Samudrasuman could say anything, he said, "O mighty king, so nice to see you. Let me have my last blessings from you. According to my horoscope, I am to receive the worst of my fate on the day I meet you in the royal gardens and will die due to it."

Samudrasuman did not realize what the priest intended to convey. He just said with a laugh, "O great sire! You always tell me not to have any superstitions, but you yourself have such beliefs, it seems. Let me keep you in front of me the whole day to see if you meet your death today."

The priest accompanied the king to the palace and sat beside him.

Hours ticked by and nothing seemed to happen to the royal priest. Samudrasuman had forgotten his own belief on that particular day. He was too preoccupied with the priest's 'horoscope'. The day seemed to pass on smoothly and the message too spread about the royal priest's "ill fated day". The priest's nephew, who was very clever, realized that there must be some reason for his uncle to spread news like that. He quickly made a plan by which he could save his uncle from the king's punishment and at the same time, remove the king's superstitious beliefs.

He walked to the palace in disguise and presented himself before Samudrasuman and said, "O king, I'm your spy posted on the border. I just came to know that your neighbouring king who has a big fleet of army is preparing to declare a war on you."

Taken aback by the news, Samudrasuman shuddered for a while with anger. Then, instead of thinking about how he could save his kingdom, he looked at the priest and called out to his soldiers. He ordered them to imprison the priest and to execute him the next day for bringing such a huge problem on him and the kingdom.

The priest listened calmly and told the king, "O my king! I am prepared for the punishment. Did I not tell you that I'm fated to die today because of seeing you in the royal gardens?"

These words hammered Samudrasuman's conscience. He realized his blunder and said to the priest in a softened tone, "O revered sire! I am extremely sorry. I have realized my mistake. It is not me who has a bad luck because of you. It is you who has got bad luck because of seeing me in the morning. So, I should be punished!"

The royal priest smiled at the king and said, "Forgive me, my lord. All the things; my words, deeds and this messenger, are false. I wanted to escape your punishment the moment I met you in the morning. So I told a lie to you and weaved a tale. My nephew understood my gesture and came to my rescue disguised as a spy. Our kingdom is not in danger, please relax."

Samudrasuman decided to overcome his superstitions and rewarded the royal priest and his nephew generously for their wisdom and courage.